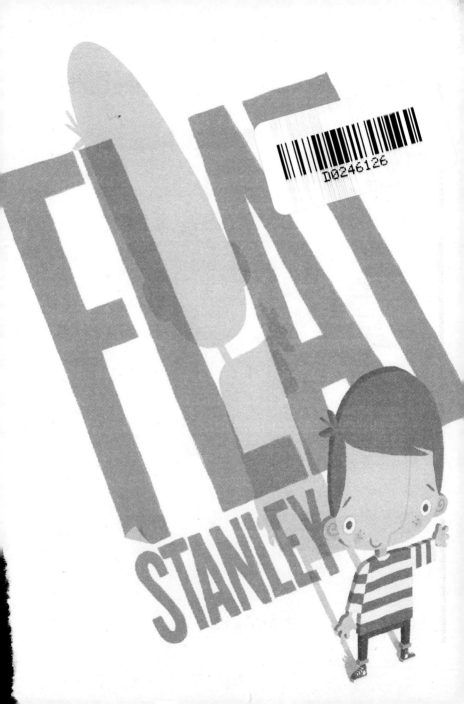

FLAT

STANLEY

READ MORE FLAT STANLEY ADVENTURES
by
JEFF BROWN

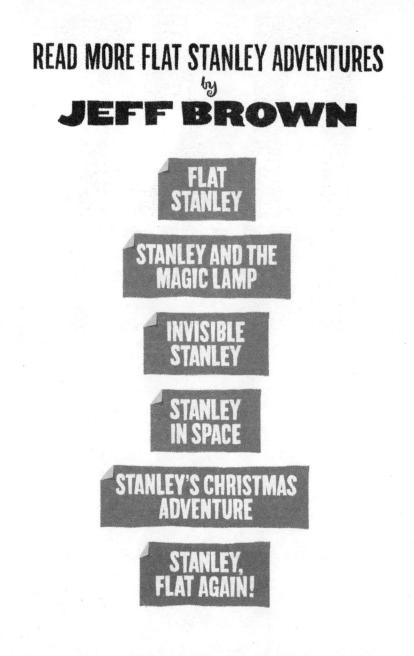

FLAT
STANLEY

STANLEY AND THE
MAGIC LAMP

INVISIBLE
STANLEY

STANLEY
IN SPACE

STANLEY'S CHRISTMAS
ADVENTURE

STANLEY,
FLAT AGAIN!

FLAT STANLEY

STANLEY'S CHRISTMAS ADVENTURE

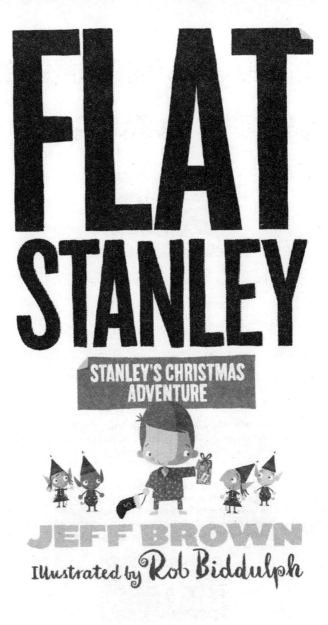

JEFF BROWN

Illustrated by Rob Biddulph

EGMONT

For Duncan
J.B

For Cash, Archie, Quinn, Clementine,
Olive, Lulu and Harley
R.B

First published in Great Britain 1985
by Methuen Children's Books Ltd
This edition published 2017
by Egmont UK Limited
The Yellow Building, 1 Nicholas Road, London W11 4AN

Text copyright © 1985 Jeff Brown
Illustrations copyright © 2017 Rob Biddulph

ISBN 978 1 4052 8808 8

www.egmont.co.uk

A CIP catalogue record for this title is available from the British Library

Printed and bound in Great Britain by the CPI Group

67675/3

CONTENTS

MEET THE
LAMBCHOP
FAMILY

STANLEY   **ARTHUR**

MRS LAMBCHOP   **MR LAMBCHOP**

THE EXTRAORDINARY STORY OF
FLAT STANLEY

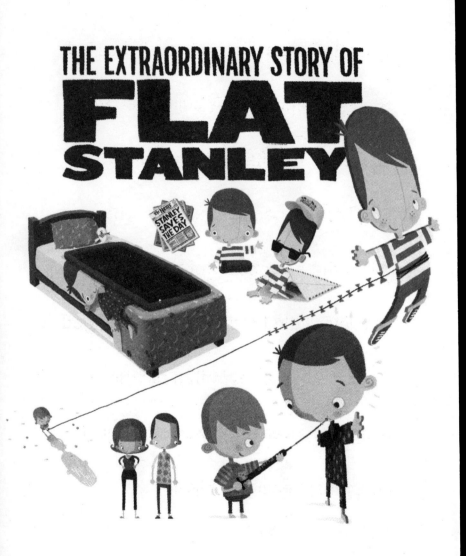

Once there was an ordinary kid called

Stanley Lambchop. A bulletin board

squashed him flat as a pancake.

Flat Stanley became famous – he even

foiled the art robbery of the century!

Stanley's little brother Arthur managed

to reinflate Stanley with a bicycle

pump, but ever since weird stuff just

keeps happening to Stanley . . .

PROLOGUE

She was the sort of little girl who liked
to be *sure* of things, so she went all over
Snow City, checking up.

The elves had done their work.

At the Post Office, Mail Elves had read
the letters, making lists of who wanted
what.

In the great workshops – the Doll
Room, the Toy Plant, the Game Mill –
Gift Elves had filled the orders, taking

care as to colour and size and style.

In the Wrap Shed the gifts lay ready, wrapped now in gay paper with holly and pine cones, sorted by country, by city or village, by road or lane or street.

The Wrap Elves teased her. 'Don't trust us, eh? . . . Snooping, we call this, Miss!'

'Pooh!' said the little girl. 'Well done, elves! Good work!'

But at home in Snow City Square, all was not well.

'Don't slam the door, dear,' said her mother, weeping. 'Your father's having his nap.'

'Mother! What's wrong?'

'He won't go this year, he says!' the mother sobbed. 'He's been so cross lately, but I never –'

'*Why*? *Why* won't he go?'

'They've lost faith, don't care any more, he says! Surely not *everyone*, I said. Think of your favourite letter, the one by your desk! He just growled at me!'

'Pooh!' said the girl. 'It's not fair! Really! I mean, everything's *ready*! Why –'

'Not now, dear,' said the mother. 'It's been a dreadful day.'

In the little office at the back of the house, the girl studied the letter her mother had mentioned, framed with others on a wall:

WORLD'S
BEST
SANTA

The girl thought for a moment, and an idea came to her. 'Hmmmm . . . Well, why not?' she said.

She looked again at the letter.

The name LAMBCHOP was printed across the top, and an address. It was signed 'Stanley, USA.'

CHAPTER 1
SARAH

It was two nights before Christmas, and all through the house not a Lambchop was stirring, but something was.

Stanley Lambchop sat up in his bed. 'Listen! Someone said "Rat".'

'It was more like "grat",' said his younger brother Arthur, from his bed. 'In the living room, I think.'

The brothers tiptoed down the stairs.

For a moment all was silence in the

darkened living room. Then came a
thump. 'Ouch!' said a small voice. 'Drat
again!'

'Are you a burglar?' Arthur called. 'Did
you hurt yourself?'

'I am *not* a burglar!' said the voice.
'Where's the – ah!' The lights came on.

The brothers stared.

Before the fireplace, by the Christmas tree, stood a slender, dark-haired little girl wearing a red jacket and skirt, both trimmed with white fur.

'I banged it *twice*,' she said, rubbing her knee. 'Coming down the chimney, and just now.'

'We *do* have a front door, you know,' said Stanley.

'Well, so does my house. But, you know, this time of year ...?' The girl sounded a bit nervous. 'Actually, I've never done this before. Let's see ... Ha, ha, ha! Season's Greetings! Ha, ha, ha!'

'"Ha, ha!" to you,' said Arthur. 'What's so funny?'

'Funny?' said the girl. 'Oh! "Ho, ho, ho!" I meant. I'm Sarah Christmas. Who are you?'

'Arthur Lambchop,' said Arthur. 'That's my brother Stanley.'

'It is? But he's not *flat.*'

'He was, but I blew him up,' Arthur explained. 'With a bicycle pump.'

'Oh, no! I wish you hadn't.' Sarah Christmas sank into a chair. 'Drat! It's all going wrong! Perhaps I shouldn't have come. But that's how I am. Headstrong, my mother says. She –'

'Excuse me,' Stanley said. 'But where are you from?'

'And why *did* you come?' said Arthur. Sarah told them.

Mr and Mrs Lambchop were reading in bed.

A tap came at the door, and then Stanley's voice. 'Hey! Can I come in?'

Mr and Mrs Lambchop cared greatly for proper speech. 'Hay is for horses, Stanley,' she said. 'And not "can" dear. You *may* come in.'

Stanley came in.

'What is the explanation, my boy, of this late call?' said Mr Lambchop, remembering past surprises. 'You have not, I see, become flat again. Has a genie come to visit? Or perhaps the President of the United States has called?'

Mrs Lambchop smiled. 'You are very amusing, George.'

'Arthur and I were in bed,' said Stanley. 'But we heard a noise and went to see. It was a girl called Sarah Christmas, from Snow City. She talks a lot. She says her father says he won't come this year, but Sarah thinks he might change his mind if I ask him to. Because I wrote him a letter once that he liked. She wants me to go with her to Snow City. In her father's sleigh. It's at the North Pole, I think.' Stanley caught his breath. 'I said I'd have to ask you first.'

'Quite right,' said Mrs Lambchop.

Mr Lambchop went to the bathroom and drank a glass of water to calm himself.

'Now then, Stanley,' he said, returning. 'You have greatly startled us. Surely —'

'Put on your robe, George,' said Mrs Lambchop. 'Let us hear for ourselves what this visitor has to say.'

'This is *delicious*!' Sarah Christmas

sipped the hot
chocolate Mrs
Lambchop had
served them
all. 'My mother
makes it too,
with cinnamon
in it. And
little cookies

with −' Her glance had fallen on the
mantelpiece. 'What's *that*, pinned up
there?'

'Christmas stockings,' Stanley said. 'The
blue one's mine.'

'But the other, the great square thing?'

'It's a pillow case.' Arthur blushed. 'My
stocking wouldn't do. I have very small
feet.'

'Pooh!' Sarah laughed. 'You wanted

extra gifts, so –'

'Sarah, dear,' Mrs Lambchop said. 'Your father? Has he truly made up his mind, you think?'

'Oh, yes!' Sarah sighed. 'But I thought – Stanley being flat, that *really* interested him. I mean, I couldn't be *sure*, but if nobody ever did anything without –'

'You seem a very nice girl, Sarah.' Mr Lambchop gave a little laugh. 'But you *have* been joking with us, surely? I –'

The phone rang, and he answered it.

'Hello, George,' the caller said. 'This is your neighbour, Frank Smith. I know it's late, but I must congratulate you on your Christmas lawn display! Best –'

'Lawn?' said Mr Lambchop. 'Display?'

'The sleigh! And those life-like *reindeer*! What makes them move about like that?

16

Batteries, I suppose?'

'Just a moment, Frank.' Mr Lambchop went to the window and looked out, Mrs Lambchop beside him.

'My goodness!' she said. 'One, two, three, four . . . eight! And such a pretty sleigh!'

Mr Lambchop returned to the phone. 'They *are* life-like, aren't they? Goodbye. Thank you for calling, Frank.'

'See? I'm not a joking kind of person, actually,' said Sarah Christmas. 'Now! My idea *might* work, even without the flatness. Do let Stanley go!'

'To the North Pole?' said Mrs Lambchop. 'At night? By himself ? Good gracious, Sarah!'

'It's not fair, asking Stanley, but not me,' said Arthur, feeling hurt. 'It's always like this! I never –'

'Oh, pooh!' Sarah Christmas smiled. 'Actually . . . You could *all* go. It's a very big sleigh.'

Mr and Mrs Lambchop looked at each other, then at Stanley and Arthur, then at each other again.

'Stanley just might make a difference, George,' Mrs Lambchop said. 'And if we can *all* go . . . ?'

'Quite right,' said Mr Lambchop. 'Sarah, we will accompany you to Snow City!'

'Hooray!' shouted Stanley and Arthur, and Sarah too.

Mrs Lambchop thought they should wait until Frank Smith had gone to bed. 'Imagine the gossip,' she said, 'were he to see our reindeer fly away.'

Mr Lambchop called his office to leave a message on the night-time answering machine. He would not be in tomorrow, he said, as he had been called unexpectedly out of town.

'There!' cried Stanley, by the window. 'The Smiths's light is out.'

The Lambchops changed quickly from pyjamas to warmer clothing, and followed Sarah to the sleigh.

CHAPTER 2
THE SLEIGH

'Welcome aboard!' said Sarah, from the driver's seat.

The Lambchops, sitting on little benches that made the big sleigh resemble a roofless bus, could scarcely contain their excitement.

The night sky shone bright with stars, and from the windows of nearby houses red and green Christmas lights twinkled over snowy lawns and streets. Before them, the eight reindeer, fur shiny in the moonlight, tossed their antlered heads.

'Ready when you are, Sarah,' Mr Lambchop said.

'Good!' Sarah cleared her throat. 'Fasten your seat belts, please! We are about to depart for Snow City. My name is Sarah – I guess you know that – and I'll be glad to answer any questions you may have. Please do not move about without permission of the Sleigh Master – that's me, at least right now – and obey whatever instructions may –'

'Puleeese!' said Arthur.

'Oh, all right!' The Lambchops fastened

their seat belts, and Sarah took up the reins. 'Ready, One? Ready, Two, Three —'

'Just *numbers*?' cried Mrs Lambchop. 'Why, we know such lovely reindeer names! Dasher, Dancer, Prancer, Vixen —'

'Comet, Cupid, Donder, Blitzen!' shouted Arthur. 'They're from a poem we know!'

'Those *are* good names!' said Sarah. 'Ready, One through Eight?'

The reindeer pawed the ground, jingling their harness bells.

'Now!' said Sarah.

The jingling stopped suddenly, and a great silence fell.

Now a silver mist rose, swirling, about the sleigh. The startled Lambchops

could see nothing beyond the mist,
not their house nor the houses of their
neighbours, not the twinkling Christmas
lights, not the bright stars above. There
was only the silver mist, everywhere, cool
against their cheeks.

'What is this, Sarah?' Mrs Lambchop called. 'Are we not to proceed to Snow City?'

Sarah's voice came cheerfully through the mist. 'We have proceeded. We're there!'

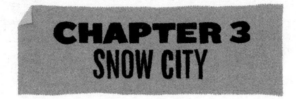

CHAPTER 3
SNOW CITY

Beyond the mist, excited voices rose. 'Sarah's back! . . . With strangers! Big ones! . . . Where's she been?'

'Poppa's elves,' said Sarah's voice. As she spoke, the mist swirled, then vanished as suddenly as it had come. Above them, the stars shone bright again.

The sleigh rested now in a snow-covered square, in front of a pretty red-roofed house. All about the square were tiny cottages, their windows aglow with light.

Elves surrounded the sleigh. 'Who are these people? . . . Is it true, what we've heard? . . . Ask Sarah! She'll know!'

The Lambchops smiled and waved. The elves seemed much like ordinary men and women, except that they had pointy ears, very wrinkled faces, and were only about half as tall as Arthur. All wore leather breeches or skirts with wide pockets

from which tools and needles stuck out.

'Miss Sarah!' came a voice. 'Is it true? He won't go this year?'

Sarah hesitated. 'Well, sort of . . . But perhaps the Lambchops here . . . Be patient. Go home, please!'

The elves straggled off toward their cottages, grumbling. 'Not going? . . . Hah! After all our work? . . . The *Who*chops? . . . I'd go work somewhere else, but where?'

A plump lady in an apron bustled out of the red-roofed house. 'Sarah! Are you all right? Going off like that! Though we did find your note. Gracious! Are those *all* Lambchops, dear?'

'I'm fine, Momma!' said Sarah. 'They wouldn't let Stanley come by himself. That's Stanley, there. The other one's Arthur. Stanley was flat, but he got round again.'

'Clever!' said Mrs Christmas. 'Well! Do all come in! Are you fond of hot chocolate?'

*

'. . . an excellent plan, I do see that. But
— Oh, he's in *such* a state! And with
Stanley no longer flat . . .' Mrs Christmas
sighed. 'More chocolate, Lambchops? I
add a dash of cinnamon. Tasty, yes?'

'Delicious,' said Mrs Lambchop.

Everyone sat silent, sipping.

Mr Lambchop felt the time had come.
'May we see him now, Mrs Christmas?
We should be getting home. So much to
do, this time of year.'

'You forget where you are, George,' said Mrs Lambchop. 'Mrs Christmas, surely, is aware of the demands of the season.'

'I'm sorry about not being flat,' Stanley said. 'I did get tired of it, though.'

'No need to apologise,' said Mrs Christmas. 'Flat, round, whatever, people must be what shape they wish.'

'So true,' said Mrs Lambchop. 'But will your husband agree?'

'We shall see. Come.' Mrs Christmas rose, and the Lambchops followed her down the hall.

Mrs Christmas knocked on a door. 'Visitors, dear! From America.'

'Send 'em back!' said a deep voice.

'Sir?' Mr Lambchop tried to sound cheerful. 'A few minutes, perhaps? "'Tis the season to be jolly", eh? We –'

'Bah!' said the voice. 'Go home!'

'What a terrible temper!' Stanley said. 'He doesn't want to meet us at all!'

'I already *have* met him once,' Arthur whispered. 'In a department store.'

'That wasn't the real one, dear,' Mrs Lambchop said.

'Too bad,' said Arthur. 'He was much nicer than this one.'

Sarah stepped forward. 'Poppa? Can you hear me, Poppa?'

'I hear you, all right!' said the deep voice. 'Took the Great Sleigh without permission, didn't you? Rascal!'

'The letter on your wall, Poppa?' Sarah said. 'The Lambchop letter? Well, they're *here*, the whole family! It wasn't easy, Poppa! I went down their chimney and scraped my knee, and then I banged it, the *same* knee, when I –'

'SARAH!' said the voice.

Sarah hushed, and so did everyone else.

'The flat boy, eh?' said the voice. 'Hmmmm . . .'

Mrs Lambchop took a comb from her bag and tidied Arthur's hair. Mr Lambchop straightened Stanley's collar.

'Come in!' said the voice behind the door.

CHAPTER 4
SARAH'S FATHER

The room was very dark, but it was possible to make out a desk at the far side, and someone seated behind it.

The Lambchops held their breaths. This was perhaps the most famous person in the world!

'Guess what, Poppa?' said Sarah, sounding quite nervous. 'The Lambchops know *names* for our reindeer!'

No answer came.

'Names, Poppa, not just *numbers*! There's Dashes and Frances and –'

'Dasher,' said Stanley. 'Then Dancer, then –'

'*Then* Frances!' cried Sarah. 'Or is it *Prances*? Then –'

'Waste of time, this!' said the figure behind the desk. But then a switch clicked, and lights came on.

The Lambchops stared.

Except for a large TV in one corner and a speaker-box on the desk, the room was much like Mr Lambchop's study at home. There were bookshelves and comfortable chairs. Framed letters, one of them Stanley's, hung behind the desk, along with photographs of Mrs Christmas, Sarah, and elves and reindeer, singly and in groups.

Sarah's father was large and stout, but otherwise not what they had expected.

He wore a blue zip jacket with 'N. Pole Athletic Club' lettered across it, and sat with his feet, in fuzzy brown slippers, up on the desk. His long white hair and beard were in need of trimming, and the beard had crumbs in it. On the desk, along with his feet, were a plate of cookies, a bowl of potato chips, and a bottle of strawberry soda with a straw in it.

'George Lambchop, sir,' said Mr Lambchop. 'Good evening. May I present my wife Harriet, and our sons Stanley and Arthur?'

'How do you do.' Sarah's father sipped his soda. 'Whichever is Stanley, step forward, please, and turn about.'

Stanley stepped forward and turned about.

'You're *round*, boy!'

'I blew him up,' said Arthur. 'With a bicycle pump.'

Sarah's father raised his eyebrows. 'Very funny. Very funny indeed.' He ate some potato chips. 'Well? What brings you all here?'

Mr Lambchop cleared his throat. 'I understand, Mr — No, that can't be right. What *is* the proper form of address?'

'Depends where you're from. "Santa" is the American way. But I'm known also as Father Christmas, *Père Noel*, *Babbo Natale*, *Julenisse* . . . Little country, way off somewhere, they call me "The Great Hugga Wagoo".'

'Hugga Wagoo?' Arthur laughed loudly,

and Mrs Lambchop shook her head at him.

Mr Lambchop continued, 'We understand, sir − *Santa*, if I may? − that you propose not to make your rounds this year? We are here to ask that you reconsider.'

'Reconsider?' said Sarah's father. 'The way things are these days? Hah! See for yourselves!'

The big TV in the corner clicked on, and he switched from channel to channel.

The first channel showed battleships firing flaming missiles; the second, aeroplanes dropping bombs; the third, cars crashing other cars. Then came buildings burning, people begging for food, people hitting each other, people firing pistols at policemen. The last channel showed a game show, men and women in chicken costumes grabbing for prizes in a pool of mud.

Sarah's father switched off the TV. 'Peace on Earth? Goodwill towards men?

Been wasting my time, it seems!'

'You have been watching *far* too much television,' said Mrs Lambchop. 'No wonder you take a dim view of things.'

'Facts are facts, madam! Everywhere, violence and greed! Hah! Right here in my own office, a whole family come begging for Christmas treats!'

The Lambchops were deeply shocked.

'I'm greedy sometimes,' said Stanley. 'But not always.'

'I'm quite nice, actually,' Arthur said. 'And Stanley's even nicer than me.'

'*I*, dear,' said Mrs Lambchop. 'Nicer than I.'

Mr Lambchop, finding it hard to believe that he was at the North Pole having a conversation like this, chose his words with care.

'You misjudge us, sir,' he said. 'There is indeed much violence in the world, and selfishness. But not everyone – we Lambchops, for example –'

'Hah! Different, are you?' Sarah's father spoke into the little box on his desk. 'Yo! Elf Ewald?'

'Central Files,' said a voice from the box. 'Ewald here.'

'Ewald,' said Sarah's father. 'Check this year's letters, under "USA". Bring me the Lambchop file.'

CHAPTER 5
THE LETTERS

Elf Ewald had come and gone, leaving behind a large brown folder.

'Not greedy, Lambchops? We shall see!' Sarah's father drew a letter from the folder and read it aloud.

'"Dear Santa, My parents say I can't have a real car until I'm grown up. I want one now. A big red one. Make that two cars, both red." Hah! Hear that? Shameful!'

Mrs Lambchop shook her head. 'I should be interested,' she said, 'to learn who wrote that letter?'

'It is signed – Hmmmm . . . Frederic. Frederic Lampop.'

Stanley laughed. 'Our name's not "Lampop"! And we don't even know any Frederics!'

'Mistakes *do* happen, you know! I get *millions* of letters!' Sarah's father drew from the folder again. 'Ah! This one's from you!'

'"Dear Santa,"' he read. '"I hope you are fine. I need lots of gifts this year. Shoes and socks and shirts and pants and underwear. And big tents. At least a hundred of each would be nice –" A hundred! *There's* greediness!'

'It does seem a bit much, Stanley,'

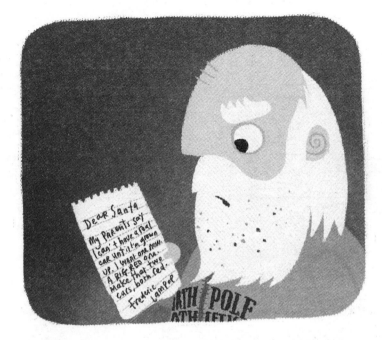

Dear Santa
My Parents say
I can't have a real
car until I'm grown
up. I want one now.
A BIG RED one.
Make that two
cars, both red.
Frederic Lambchop

said Mr Lambchop. 'And why tents, for goodness sake?'

'You'll see,' said Stanley.

Sarah's father read on. '". . . of each would be nice. But not delivered to my house. It was on TV about a terrible earthquake in South America where all the houses fell down, and people lost all

47

their clothes and don't have anywhere to live. Please take everything to where the earthquake was. Thank you. Your friend, Stanley Lambchop. PS. I would send my old clothes, but they are mostly from when I was flat and wouldn't fit anybody else.'"

'Good for you, Stanley!' said Mrs Lambchop. 'A fine idea, the tents.'

'Hmmmph! One letter, that's all.' Sarah's father chose another letter. 'This one's got jam on it.'

'Excuse me,' said Arthur. 'I was eating a sandwich.'

'"Dear Santa,"' Sarah's father read, '"I have hung up a pillow case instead of a stocking −" Hah! The old pillow case trick!'

'Wait!' cried Arthur. 'Read the rest!'

'". . . instead of a stocking. Please fill this up with chocolate bars, my favourite kind with nuts. My brother Stanley is writing to you about an earthquake, and how people there need clothes and tents and things. Well, I think they need food too, and little stoves to cook on. So please give them the chocolate bars, and food and stoves. The bars should be the big kind. It doesn't matter about the nuts. Sincerely, Arthur Lambchop."'

Mrs Lambchop gave Arthur a little hug.

'All right, *two* letters,' said Sarah's father. 'But from brothers. Count as one, really.'

He took a last letter from the folder. 'Nice penmanship, this one . . . Mr and Mrs George Lambchop! Now there's a surprise!'

'Well, why *not*?' said Mrs Lambchop.

Mr Lambchop said, 'No harm, eh, just dropping a line?'

Their letter was read.

'"Dear Sir: Perhaps you expect letters from children only, since as people grow older they often begin to doubt that you truly exist. But when our two sons were very small, and asked if you were real, we said "yes". And if they were to ask again now, we would not say "no". We would say that you are not real, of course, for those who do not believe in you, but very real indeed for those who do. Our Christmas wish is that you will never have cause to doubt that Stanley and Arthur Lambchop, and their parents, take the latter position. Sincerely, Mr and Mrs George Lambchop, USA."'

Sarah's father thought for a moment.
'Hmmm ... *Latter* position? Ah? *Do* believe.
I see.'

'See, Poppa?' said Sarah. 'No
greediness! Not one —'

'Fine letters, Sarah. I agree.' There was
sadness in the deep voice now. 'But all,
Sarah, from the same family that thought
to deceive me with that "flatness" story.

Flat indeed!'

Mrs Lambchop gasped. 'Deceive? Oh, no!'

'Round is round, madam.' Sarah's father shook his head. 'The lad's shape speaks for itself.'

The hearts of all the Lambchops sank within them. Their mission had failed, they thought. For millions and millions of children all over the world, a joyful holiday was lost, perhaps never to come again.

Arthur felt especially bad. It was his fault, he told himself, for thinking of that bicycle pump.

Stanley felt worst of all. If only he hadn't grown tired of being flat, hadn't let Arthur blow him round again! If only there were proof –

And then he remembered something.

'Wait!' he shouted, and stood on tiptoe to whisper in Mrs Lambchop's ear. 'What . . .?' she said. 'I can't – The *what*? Oh! Yes! I had forgotten! Good for you, Stanley!'

Rummaging in her bag, she found her wallet, from which she drew a photograph. She gave it to Sarah's father.

'Do keep that,' she said. 'We have more at home.'

The snapshot had been taken by Mr

Lambchop the day after the big bulletin board fell on Stanley. It showed him, quite flat, sliding under a closed door. Only his top half was visible, smiling up at the camera. The bottom half was still behind the door.

For a long moment, as Sarah's father studied the picture, no one spoke.

'My apologies, Lambchops,' he said at

last. 'Flat he is. *Was*, anyhow. I've half a mind to –' He sighed. 'But those red cars, asking for *two*, that –'

'That was Lam*POP*!' cried Arthur. 'Not –'

'Just teasing, lad!'

Sarah's father had jumped up, a great smile on his face.

'Yo, elves!' he shouted into his speaker phone. 'Prepare to load gifts! Look lively! Tomorrow is Christmas Eve, you know!'

The next moments were joyful indeed.

'Thank you, thank you! . . . Hooray! . . . Hooray! . . . Hooray!' shouted Mr and Mrs Lambchop, and Stanley and Arthur and Sarah.

Sarah's mother kissed everyone. Mrs Lambchop kissed Sarah's father, and almost fainted when she realised what she had done.

Then Sarah's father asked Stanley to autograph the sliding-under-the-door picture, and when Stanley had written 'All best wishes, S. Lambchop' across the picture, he pinned it to the wall.

'Blew him round, eh?' he said to Arthur. 'Like to have seen that!'

He turned to Sarah. 'Come, my dear! While I freshen up, teach me those reindeer names. Then I will see our visitors safely home!'

CHAPTER 6
GOING HOME

A crowd of elves had gathered with Mrs
Christmas and Sarah to say goodbye.
'Bless you, Lambchops!' they called.
'Thank goodness you came! . . . Think
if you hadn't! . . . Whew! . . . Farewell,
farewell!'

In the Great Sleigh, Sarah's father took
up the reins. 'Ready, Lambchops?'

He made a fine appearance now, his
hair and beard combed, and wearing a

smart green cloak and cap. The famous red suit, he had explained, was reserved for delivering gifts.

'Goodbye, everyone!' called Mrs Lambchop. 'We will remember you always!'

'You bet!' cried Stanley. 'I'll *never* forget!'

'But you will, dear,' said Mrs Christmas. 'You will *all* forget.'

'Hardly.' Mr Lambchop smiled. 'An evening like this does not slip one's mind.'

'Poppa will see to it, actually,' said Sarah. 'Snow City, all of us here . . . We're supposed to be, you know, sort of a mystery. Isn't that *silly*? I mean, if –'

'Sarah!' her father said. 'We must go.'

The Lambchops looked up at the night

sky, still bright with stars, then turned for a last sight of the little red-roofed house behind them, and of the elves' cottages about the snowy square.

'We are ready,' said Mr Lambchop.

'Goodbye, goodbye!' called Mrs Lambchop and Stanley and Arthur.

'Goodbye, goodbye!' called the elves, waving.

The eight reindeer tossed their heads, jingling their harness bells. One bell flew off, and Stanley caught the little silver cup in his hand. Suddenly, as before, the jingling stopped, all was silence, and the pale mist rose again about the sleigh.

Sarah's father's voice rang clear. 'Come, Dasher, Dancer, Prancer, Vixen! Come, Comet, Cupid, Donder and . . . oh, whatsisname?'

'Blitzen!' Stanley called.

'Thank you. Come, Blitzen!'

The mist swirled, closing upon the sleigh.

CHAPTER 7
CHRISTMAS

The Lambchops all remarked the next morning on how soundly they had slept, and how late. Mr Lambchop ate breakfast in a rush.

'Will you be all day at the office, George?' Mrs Lambchop asked. 'It *is* Christmas Eve, you know.'

'There is much to do,' said Mr Lambchop. 'I will be kept late, I'm afraid.'

But there was little to occupy him at

his office, since a practical joker had left word he would not be in. He was home by noon to join friends and family for carol singing about the neighbourhood.

Mrs Lambchop had the carollers in for hot chocolate, which was greatly admired. She had added cinnamon, she explained; the idea had just popped into her head. The carollers were all very jolly, and Frank Smith, who lived next door, made everyone laugh, the Lambchops hardest of all, by claiming he had seen reindeer on their lawn the night before.

On Christmas morning, they opened their gifts to each other, and gifts from relatives and friends. Then came a surprise for Stanley and Arthur. Mr Lambchop had just turned on the TV news.

'. . . and now a flash from South America, from where the earthquake was,' the announcer was saying. 'Homeless villagers here are giving

thanks this morning for a tremendous supply of socks, shirts, underwear, and food. They have also received a *thousand* tents, and a *thousand* little stoves to cook on!' The screen showed a homeless villager, looking grateful. 'The tents, and the little stoves,' the villager said. 'Just what we need! Bless whoever sends these tents and stoves! Also the many tasty chocolate bars with nuts!'

'He's blessing *me*!' cried Stanley. 'I asked for tents in my letter. But I wasn't sure it would work.'

'Well, I wrote about stoves,' Arthur said. '*And* chocolate bars. But they didn't have to have nuts.'

Happy coincidences! thought Mr and Mrs Lambchop, smiling at each other.

Christmas dinner, shared with various

aunts, uncles, and cousins, was an
enormous meal of turkey, yams, and
three kinds of pie. Then everyone went